Hello, Family Members,

Learning to read is one of the most important accomplishments of early childhood. **Hello Reader!** books are designed to help children become skilled readers who like to read. Beginning readers learn to read by remembering frequently used words like "the," "is," and "and"; by using phonics skills to decode new words; and by interpreting picture and text clues. These books provide both the stories children enjoy and the structure they need to read fluently and independently. Here are suggestions for helping your child *before*, *during*, and *after* reading:

Before

- Look at the cover and pictures and have your child predict what the story is about.
- Read the story to your child.
- Encourage your child to chime in with familiar words and phrases.
- Echo read with your child by reading a line first and having your child read it after you do.

During

- Have your child think about a word he or she does not recognize right away. Provide hints such as "Let's see if we know the sounds" and "Have we read other words like this one?"
- Encourage your child to use phonics skills to sound out new words.
- Provide the word for your child when more assistance is needed so that he or she does not struggle and the experience of reading with you is a positive one.
- Encourage your child to have fun by reading with a lot of expression . . . like an actor!

After

- Have your child keep lists of interesting and favorite words.
- Encourage your child to read the books over and over again. Have him or her read to brothers, sisters, grandparents, and even teddy bears. Repeated readings develop confidence in young readers.
- Talk about the stories. Ask and answer questions. Share ideas about the funniest and most interesting characters and events in the stories.

I do hope that you and your child enjoy this book.

—Francie Alexander
Reading Specialist,
Scholastic's Learning Ventures

For Megan and Sean
— F.R.

To all our animal neighbors
who share this ride
around the sun
— J.C.

Special thanks to Laurie Roulston
of the Denver Museum of Natural History
for her expertise

ISBN: 0-439-06754-5

Text copyright © 2000 by Fay Robinson.
Illustrations copyright © 2000 by Jean Cassels.
All rights reserved. Published by Scholastic Inc.
SCHOLASTIC, HELLO READER, CARTWHEEL BOOKS and associated logos are trademarks and/or registered trademarks of Scholastic Inc.

Library of Congress Cataloging-in-Publication Data

Robinson, Fay.
    Creepy beetles / by Fay Robinson; illustrated by Jean Cassels.
        p.   cm. — (Hello reader! Science — Level 2)
"Cartwheel Books."
    Summary: Simple rhyming text describes the many different ways beetles can look and how they behave, from sparkling to hairy, from hiking to flying.
    ISBN: 0-439-06754-5
    1. Beetles—Juvenile literature.   [1. Beetles.]   I. Title. II. Series.
III. Cassels, Jean, ill.
QL576.2 .R63   2000
595.76 21—dc21

99-041767
CIP
AC

10 9 8 7 6 5 4 3

00 01 02 03 04

Printed in the U.S.A.

24

First printing, May 2000

Creepy Beetles!

by Fay Robinson
Illustrated by Jean Cassels

Hello Reader! Science — Level 2

Cartwheel
·B·O·O·K·S·®

SCHOLASTIC INC.

New York   Toronto   London   Auckland   Sydney
Mexico City   New Delhi   Hong Kong

Beetles here,

beetles there,

beetles creeping everywhere!

Strolling in the frosty snow,

jungle branches, high

and low.

Beetles hiking desert land,
leaving bug tracks in the sand.

Beetles crept in days of yore.
Beetles lived with dinosaurs.

Beetles can look very cool —
sparkling like a fancy jewel.

Great designs and awesome spots.
Shiny red with jet black dots.

Pretty beetles.

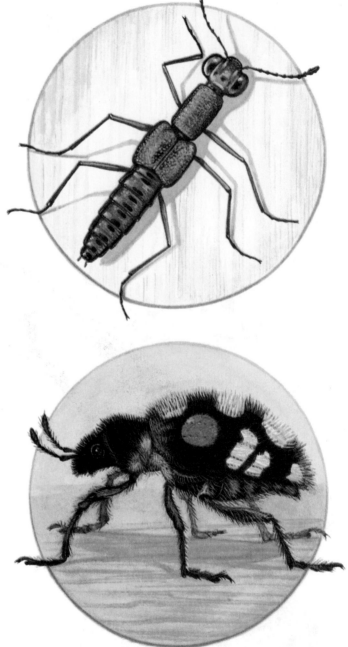

Hairy beetles.

Really, really scary beetles.

Some that look
like little tents,

turtles,

spiders,

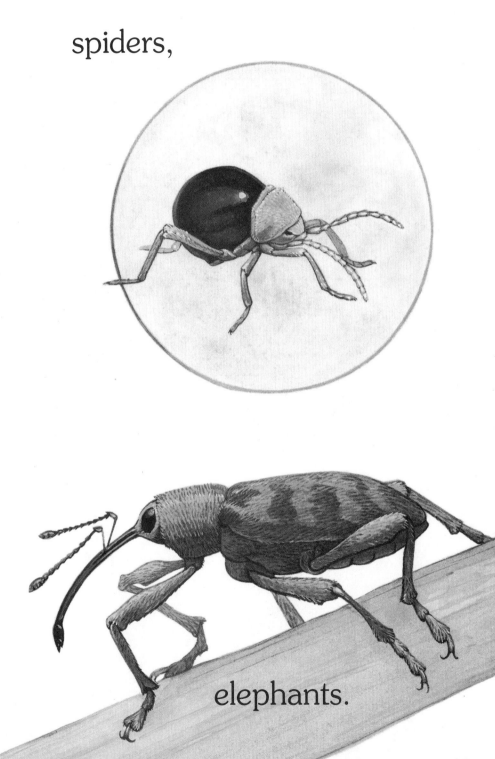

elephants.

Beetles start as little eggs.
Soon they hatch —
worms with legs!

These worms, called larvae,
eat with zest.
When they're done,
they stop and rest.

Safe and snug and very still,
they change, and grow,
and change until,

a grown-up beetle pushes out,
dries, and starts to creep about.

Beetles dine on stems and leaves,

all the tasty parts of trees,

flower petals, other bugs.

Carpet beetles eat our rugs!

Diving beetles, if they wish,
might enjoy a yummy fish.

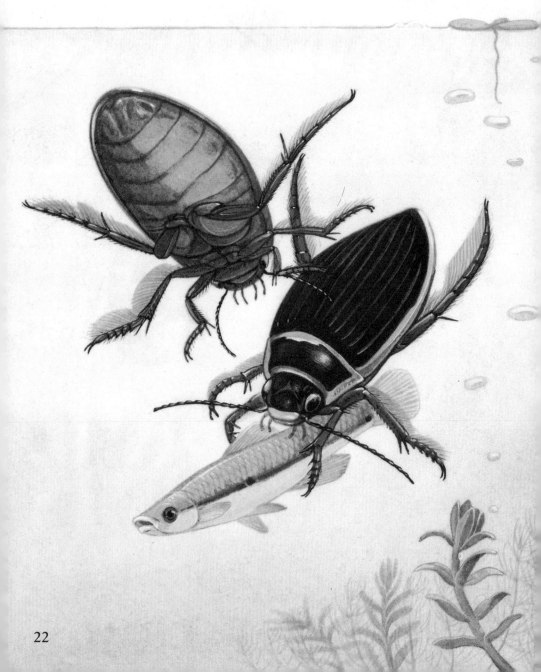

A beetle, when it wants to fly,
spreads its hidden wings.
Goodbye!

Beetles whirling 'round
and 'round.

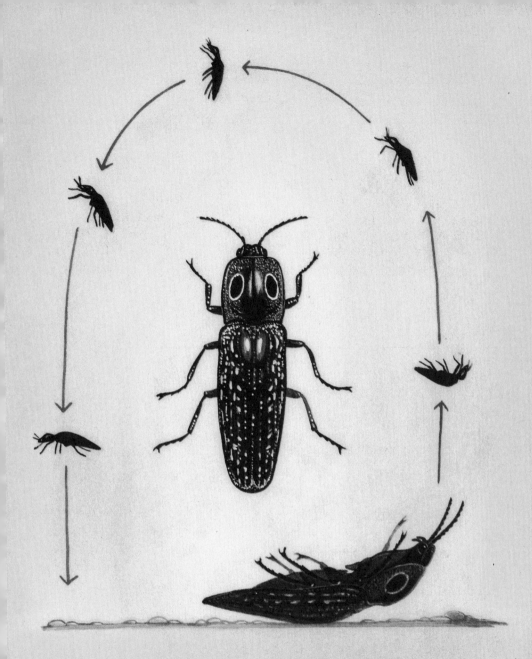

Beetles flipping off the ground.

Beetle battles. What a sight!

Beetles lighting up the night.

Beetles here, beetles there,

beetles creeping everywhere!

Cover: Cardinal Beetle

Cover: Blister Beetle

Cover:
Milkweed Leaf Beetle

Cover: Lady Beetle

Cover: Cockchafer

Page 4: Laurel Borer

Page 4:
Milkweed Beetle

Page 4:
Striped Blister Beetle

Page 4: Caterpillar
Hunter Ground Beetle

Page 4: Northern
Carrion Beetle

Page 5: Elder Borer

Page 5:
Red Milkweed Beetle

Page 5:
Purple Fungus Beetle

Page 5:
Shining Fungus Beetle

Page 6: Soldier Beetle

Page 7: Stag Beetle

Page 8: Broad-necked
Darkling Beetle

Page 9:
Lamellicorn Beetle

Page 9:
Ground Beetle

Page 10: Wood Borer

Page 11:
Harlequin Beetle

Page 11: Lady Beetle

Page 12: Rove Beetle

Page 12: Snout Beetle

Page 13:
Hercules Beetle

Page 14:
Tortoise Beetles

Page 15: Spider Beetle

Page 15: Snout Beetle

Page 16:
Lady Beetle larvae

Page 17: Lady Beetle
larvae eating aphids

Page 17:
Lady Beetle pupa

Page 18:
Lady Beetle pupa

Page 19: Lady Beetle

Page 20:
Colorado Potato Beetle

Page 20:
Cottonwood Borer

Page 21: Rose Weevil

Page 21: Tiger Beetle

Page 21: Carpet Beetle

Page 22:
Water Beetles

Page 23:
Cardinal Beetle

Page 24:
Whirligig Beetle

Page 25: Click Beetle

Page 26: Stag Beetle

Page 27: Firefly

Page 28: Green Scarab

Page 28:
Checkered Beetle

Page 28: Gold and
Turquoise Leaf Beetle

Page 28:
Gold Tortoise Beetle

Page 28: Ground Beetle

Page 29: Cockchafer

Page 29: Cockchafer

Page 29: Red-headed
Cardinal Beetle

Page 29:
Bronze Potato Beetle

Page 29: South
American Weevil

Page 29: Tortoise Beetle

Page 29:
Mexican Leaf Beetle